BEAR

BLACKWINGS
DEVIL SPRINGS

TEAGAN BROOKS

BEAR

BLACKWINGS MC - DEVIL SPRINGS - BOOK SIX

TEAGAN BROOKS

BLURB

After spending sixteen years behind bars for brutally murdering the man who killed my wife, I was released earlier than expected thanks to my daughter-in-law. I never resented my time in prison. I knew what I was doing from the moment his first drop of blood fell, until I turned myself in days later.

I was thrilled to be back home with what was left of my friends and family, though I wasn't sure where I'd fit in after being gone so long. I shouldn't have worried. My brothers are my brothers for a reason. After the initial welcome home party, they carried on as if I'd always been there.

Life was good. I was content. Wasn't wanting for anything. Then, a little girl asked me if she could have a flower from my wife's grave, and she stole my heart. Little did I know, so would her mother.

ISBN: 978-1-951704-21-6

Cover Designer: CT Cover Creations

To my dear friend Merin.

PROLOGUE

"What the fuck is this?" I yelled and shoved the paper into Sean's face.

He snatched it from my hand and scanned over it, confirming my fear with the narrowing of his eyebrows. "It looks like an eviction notice," he sighed. "We knew it was coming."

"Yeah, but not this soon! What are we going to do?"

Sean shrugged. "Not much of shit we can do."

"You know, you could try to help me here," I huffed. "Why do I have to do everything?"

"Because I don't fucking want to."

I turned to him and smiled. "Okay, have it your way."

"What's that supposed to mean?"

"It means once I get this figured out, and I will, you'll be out on your ass."

"This is my place."

"You and I both know that's bullshit."

"My name's on the lease," he countered.

"Well then, that would make you responsible for everything in here," I said and paused to cross my arms over my chest. "It'd be a shame if someone got wind of what you've got going on in here."

"Wait, I think you misunderstood," he backpedaled.

"I don't take care of other people. They take care of me. Remember that."

"You're taking care of my dad," he said, sounding like a petulant brat.

"So he can take care of me!" I yelled in frustration.

"Look," he said and held his palms up. "I don't know what to do, but if you think of something, I'll help. As long as our other arrangement doesn't change."

"It won't if we stay here, but you aren't fucking this high-maintenance pussy on your friend's mom's couch." Instead of waiting for his response, I winked and closed the bedroom door behind me.

Flopping onto the bed, I covered my eyes with my arm. Once again, I had all sorts of problems to deal with because of someone else's fuck up, and I was running out of time to come up with a plan. But I'd worked too hard to get where I was to let it all be taken away without a fight.

We needed cash, and we needed it fast. But I didn't have anything to work with. When the cops showed up and raided our home, anything of value that wasn't confiscated for the investigation was destroyed during their search. We didn't even have a working television to watch.

The quiet was driving me crazy. Anything would've been better than the deafening silence. A bouncing basketball. A barking dog. A crying baby.

I was on the verge of ripping my hair out when Sean pushed his way into my bedroom. "I forgot to tell you. My dad called earlier to remind you to put new flowers on Grandfather's grave."

"Fuck," I groaned. I'd completely forgotten about the mundane task. It was a waste of time and money, but it was the only thing Carter asked me to do for him while he was away, and I needed to keep up appearances. So, I begrudgingly got to my feet to go out and find some festive fake flowers for the dead.

"You're coming with me. You can drive."

"I'll pass."

"I wasn't asking. Get in the fucking car."

"You're such a bitch."

I gasped in mock offense. "Me? A bitch? Never."

1

MACKENZIE

The first time I saw him, he was kneeling beside a headstone a few plots down from my late husband's. I wasn't staring at him, but it felt like I'd been caught when he looked up and his dark green eyes locked with mine.

I'd heard about him before and recognized him instantly. But I'd never seen him in person. And he was a sight to behold. Tall and handsome, covered in muscles and leather, looking like a dark angel next to the grave. For a split second, I froze as an unfamiliar feeling shot through me. One I hadn't felt since before Russell died.

"Hello!" my three-year-old daughter called, waving excitedly as she walked toward him. "I like your pretty flowers."

"Freeze!" I ordered in a harsh tone—the one I reserved for urgent situations—like when she approached an unknown person.

Brinkley was a friendly child, and that scared the

shit out of me because, to her, everyone she met was a potential new friend—regardless of their age.

Thankfully, she was also an obedient child and stopped at the sound of my voice. Then, she waited for me to take her hand before she continued toward her target. By that time, he had risen to his feet and was watching us with a curious smile.

"Hello, Mister! I like your pretty flowers. My name's Brinkley Moore. I'm three years old. I like pigs. And this is my mommy, Mackenzie Moore. We live in Devil Springs. Her phone number is nine—"

"Hold on, Brinkley," I interrupted before she could finish giving out my phone number to a stranger. Again.

After finding a lost child at the mall while we were Christmas shopping the year before, I taught Brinkley my phone number and how to call me in case she ever got lost. Never in a million years did I think she would proceed to recite my number along with my full name and hers every time she said hello to a stranger in public. But that's exactly what happened, and I'd been coming up with creative ways to interrupt her ever since.

I turned my attention to him. "I'm so sorry for disturbing you. Please excuse us. We'll be on our way."

"No apologies necessary," he smiled kindly. "Can she have one? A flower?"

"Oh, uh, sure," I said and looked down at my daughter. "Would you like a flower?"

"Yes, please!" she squealed.

"One," I said firmly. "And be sure to say thank you."

"Okay, Mommy."

"I do apologize for interrupting your visit," I said once we were standing beside him. "She's too young to understand where we are."

And while that was true, I'd always wondered if Brinkley understood more about where we were in a way that I couldn't. The first time Brinkley smiled was during one of our visits with Russell. From then on, whenever we went to the cemetery or drove past a graveyard, she would giggle and laugh. But after she started walking and talking, things got even more strange. When we took flowers to Russell's grave, she would toddle to a nearby headstone, sit down, and begin babbling as if she were having a conversation with someone.

"She's fine," he said and bent down to help Brinkley get a flower. "Which one do you want?"

Brinkley wobbled as she squatted down and placed her hands on her knees to study the flowers before making her selection. "This one," she said and straightened to point out her choice. "Thank you, Mister. Look, Mommy, it's Mystical's favorite."

"It's very pretty," I said slowly, trying to figure out who or what she was talking about.

"Will you put it in my hair, please? Right here?" she asked and pointed above her ear.

"Let me see if I have a hair thingy. Oh, this might work." Pulling a small hair clip from my purse, I tucked the stem behind her ear and secured it into place.

Brinkley turned around with a broad smile on her face. "Thank you for the pretty flower, Mister."

"You're welcome, Brinkley," he said and turned his attention to me. "And Mackenzie, right?"

"Yes," I nodded and extended my hand. "And you must be Bear, Batta's dad."

He blinked in surprise before he grinned proudly. "I am. How'd you know?"

"I've heard him mention you before," I said and nodded toward the name displayed on his chest, "and you look just like him."

"Can't deny that one bit. So, how do you know my son?"

"I'm friends with Coal," I said.

"Coal is my babysitter!" Brinkley announced.

"He is?" Bear chuckled.

"Yes! He plays hide and seek with me. Mommy, can Coal come over to play today?"

"Not today. We're making Christmas goodies tonight."

Bear was still chuckling. "I'm sorry, but I've got to know how Coal became your babysitter."

"Brinkley was around nine months old the first time we went to the clubhouse. As an infant, she didn't like anyone other than me. Until we met Coal," I smiled at the memory. "After I made a joke about him being a biker babysitter, he told me to call him if I ever needed one. When I came down with a stomach virus a few months later, I was too sick to take care of Brinkley. So, I called Coal for help, and here we are."

"Sounds like Coal. He's a good kid."

"Mommy! I gotta go potty!" Brinkley shouted and crossed her legs for emphasis.

"Okay, sweetie," I replied automatically and reached for her hand. "I'm sorry to rush off. I don't have much time on the clock that just started ticking. But it was nice talking to you."

"Bye, Mr. Bear. Bye, Mystical," Brinkley waved.

2

BEAR

"Nice talking with you, too," I said and waved goodbye to Mackenzie and her daughter as they hurried back to her car.

I'm not sure why I kept my eyes on them, but I was glad I did. Otherwise, I wouldn't have seen the only other vehicle in the lot leave right after Mackenzie did.

I noticed the car arrive shortly after Mackenzie and didn't think anything of it at first. But after over a decade in prison, it was second nature to pay close attention to my surroundings. So, I also noticed that no one got out of the vehicle.

I'd planned on staying to visit with Nicole for a while longer but decided it wouldn't hurt anything to cut my time short and follow the car. It was likely nothing, but I'd taken my chance with likely before, and it didn't end in my favor.

Mackenzie turned into a grocery store parking lot

a few miles down the road. As did the person I suspected was following her.

Parking near the rear entrance, I kept my eyes on the sedan. To my surprise, it circled the lot once before turning out onto the road and driving away.

"Wasn't expecting that," I mumbled to myself when the excitement I'd been gearing up for came to a sudden halt.

Since I was already there, I went inside to pick up a few things I needed. At least, that's what I told myself as I entered the store. It had nothing to do with the beautiful, captivating woman and her charismatic daughter I'd just met.

"Mr. Bear!" Brinkley shouted when she saw me—which took far longer than it should have for either of them to notice me. Something I wanted to mention once I figured out how to do so without it coming across as offensive, or creepy.

"Hello, Miss Brinkley," I said and pretended to be surprised to see them. "Are you helping Mommy shop?"

"Yes," she said proudly. "We're making Christmas goodies."

"You are? That sounds like fun."

"Mommy! Can Mr. Bear come over and make Christmas goodies with us?" she asked, yelling her question for everyone in the vicinity to hear.

"I don't know," Mackenzie said. "You'll have to ask him."

"Do you want to make Christmas goodies with us?" Brinkley asked excitedly.

"I'm afraid I can't tonight, but thank you for inviting me." I didn't have any plans, but I didn't want to put Mackenzie in an awkward position.

"You're welcome. Merry Christmas, Mr. Bear!"

"Merry Christmas," Mackenzie and I said at the same time.

"Bye, Mr. Bear!" Brinkley waved, and continued to do so until Mackenzie turned the corner to the next aisle. "Bye!" she shouted one last time.

I chuckled to myself and made my way to the registers, smiling broadly from her upbeat and contagious energy. But then I found myself slightly disappointed that I was headed home alone instead of going to make Christmas goodies with them.

As I carried my few bags of groceries out to my bike, I wondered what had gotten into me. Or rather, what was wrong with me. My gut feelings and intuitions were rarely, if ever, wrong. Hell, following one of my feelings was how I ended up in prison.

I put my bags in the side compartments and got on my bike before pulling my helmet on. I was just about to start my bike and leave when my eyes flicked to where Mackenzie had parked. Then to a white sedan a few spaces down from her. The same fucking car I thought was following her. The one I watched circle the parking lot and leave. The one that must've returned while we were in the store.

Yanking my helmet off, I held it in my hand and walked toward the vehicle with purpose. I had every intention of speaking to the driver through their window, after it was opened in one way or another.

However, the fucker pulled forward through the space and drove away before I could reach them. But not before I got the license plate number.

As I passed Mackenzie's car on the way back to my bike, I turned around when something caught my eye. After taking a second glance, I realized her rear passenger tire was almost flat. So instead of going back inside to find her, I waited for her and Brinkley to come out of the store so I could offer to change it for her.

"Hello, again, Mr. Bear," Brinkley waved excitedly while she announced my presence.

"Hello," I smiled and returned her wave before directing my attention to Mackenzie. "I hate to be the bearer of bad news, but you've got a flat," I said and pointed to the tire.

She looked down and scrunched her nose. "Crap," she said softly before turning back to me. "Thanks for letting me know."

"If you've got a spare, I can change it for you."

"I appreciate it, but I have a number to call to have someone come out and fix it," she said and held up a card attached to her keys.

"You sure?" I asked. "You'll probably have to wait at least an hour before anyone can get here," I said and nodded my head toward her daughter. "I can have you two on your way in less than twenty minutes."

She glanced at Brinkley, who was quietly playing with a toy in the shopping cart. "An hour is a long time for her."

"Is that a yes?"

"If you're sure it's not too much trouble."

"It's not. This isn't the first flat I've changed, and it won't be the last."

"Thank you all the same. What do you need me to do?"

I pointed to my bike near the back of the lot. "Can you move your car over there? It'll be out of the way, and I'll have more room to work."

"It's okay to drive it over there?" she asked worriedly.

"As long as you go slow, it'll be fine."

It only took me fifteen minutes to change her tire and have her ready to go. However, I took my time loading the flat into her trunk when I noticed the white sedan pulling into a parking space across the street. I watched them for a few minutes before I went to let Mackenzie know I was finished.

"Thank you so much, Bear," Mackenzie said with her hands tightly clasped together.

"No problem," I said and glanced at her hands. "You okay?"

"Uh, yeah," she answered distractedly, with her eyes focused on something in the distance. I turned and followed the direction of her gaze to the car across the street. "I've never driven with a spare, but it should be pretty much the same as regular driving, right?"

I didn't think that was what she was nervous about, but I played along to see what would happen.

"For the most part. Do you want me to follow you home in case you have any trouble?" I offered.

"Oh, no. I'll be fine."

But something told me she was being polite. I didn't want to push her or make her uncomfortable, so I decided to try once more before letting it go. "It'd make me feel better if I at least make sure you get home okay."

"I think I would too," she said so quietly I almost didn't hear her, and wasn't sure I heard her correctly.

"Thank you," she smiled. "I don't live too far from here."

I followed her the few miles down the road to her house and pulled into her driveway behind her to turn around.

Then, the white sedan drove by her house.

Instead of going home, I rode right into Mackenzie's garage and parked my bike beside her car.

"Do you know them?" I asked, pointing toward the road even though the car was no longer visible.

Mackenzie's face paled. "I thought it was me."

"Thought what was?"

"The car. I thought I was being paranoid. I keep seeing it, and no, I don't know them," she admitted.

"When did you first notice it?"

Her answer made my stomach drop. "The first time was a few days ago."

I don't know why I'd assumed this was the first time the car followed her, but I had, which was why her answer surprised me. "Days?"

"Yes," she confirmed. "I saw it in the parking garage at the mall a few days ago. Then, later the same day, I saw it drive by my house, twice. And today at the grocery store." She shrugged. "It's probably a new neighbor, and I'm reading too much into it."

"There's nothing wrong with being aware of your surroundings," I said and wondered if she had indeed seen me at the store.

"When did you notice it?" she asked.

"At the cemetery. They left right after you did."

"What?" she whispered and covered her chest with her hand.

"Mommy! Buckle me out," Brinkley sang from inside the car.

"Just a minute, sweetie," Mackenzie said and turned her attention back to me. "I need to get her and the groceries inside. Would you like to come in for a cup of coffee or something to drink? I feel like we should talk about this car a little more."

"Sounds good to me." While she got Brinkley out of her car seat, I gathered her bags of groceries and carried them into the house behind her.

"Mommy, can Mr. Bear make goodies with us?" Brinkley asked again.

"We'll see. How about you go find your apron while I put the groceries away."

"Okay. Be right back."

"The car was at the cemetery?" Mackenzie asked as soon as Brinkley was out of earshot.

"Yes," I confirmed. "It arrived shortly after you

did. No one got out, and they pulled out behind you when you left."

"Is that why you were following me around the grocery store?"

I shrugged. "Pretty much. I didn't want to alarm you if it was nothing, but I didn't want to ignore it if it wasn't."

"Thank you," she said. "I wouldn't have stopped at the store with Brinkley if I'd seen them."

"I got their tag number. Do you want me to find out who it is?" I asked, knowing I was going to regardless of her answer.

"Is that something you can do easily?" she returned.

"Very."

"Then, yes, I'd like to know."

"I'll see what I can find out," I told her and sent a text to Spazz with the tag number.

"Would you like a cup of coffee or something else to drink?"

"I'll never say no to a cup of coffee."

"Me either," she smiled and started the coffee before she put away her groceries.

A few minutes later, Brinkley returned and climbed into the chair beside me. "I'm ready, Mommy."

"Do you want to pick out our first Christmas movie while I get things ready in here?"

"Yes!" she shouted and climbed down from her seat. "But don't start without me."

"I won't," Mackenzie promised.

"She's something else," I laughed.

"She keeps me on my toes. Cream or sugar?"

"Heavy on both."

Mackenzie smiled. A genuine smile that lit up her entire face. "That's how I like mine, too."

When she placed my cup in front of me, I arched an eyebrow as I lifted it to my mouth. "Now, the real question is, do we like it the same strength?" I took a tentative sip and subsequently groaned.

Mackenzie laughed. "That sounds like a yes."

My phone dinged with a text from Spazz.

"The car belongs to Carter Perry," I told Mackenzie.

"Carter Perry," she repeated. "I don't recognize the name."

Bear: The name doesn't seem familiar. Can you find some more info?

Spazz: Sure.

Bear: Thanks, brother.

"I asked him to pull some information. See if we can find out why you're seeing him so much."

"I appreciate it," she said sincerely, then lowered her voice. "She's going to be hungry soon. I was going to order a pizza. Would you like to stay for dinner?"

Maybe it was my own wishful thinking, but it

sounded like she didn't want me to leave. And I wanted to stay.

"Who can say no to pizza?"

"Not me!" Brinkley shouted. "Mommy! Can we have pizza?"

"Well," Mackenzie said slowly, pretending to consider her request. "I don't know. Do we deserve a treat?"

"We always deserve treats!" Brinkley sang.

"Okay, I'll order pizza, and we'll start the Christmas goodies after dinner."

"Thank you, Mommy," she said happily and danced all the way down the hall while singing, "Pizza, pizza, pizza."

3

MACKENZIE

Brinkley went to her room to play while we waited for the pizza to arrive, leaving me alone in the kitchen with Bear. Surprisingly, I didn't feel the slightest bit uncomfortable with him in my house, even though I didn't know him or know anything about him.

Well, I wasn't scared or worried he might hurt me. I was, however, very aware of his presence. Bear was a large man who couldn't be overlooked due to his sheer size alone. Not only that, Bear had this distinguished yet rugged look to him, and every part of my vagina wanted to tell him how well he was rocking it.

I turned when I heard Bear's phone sound with a text message. He stared at the screen for several moments before he looked up with a furrowed brow.

"Is something wrong?"

"Uh, no," he started. "Spazz is requesting more

information, and to be perfectly honest, it's a little invasive."

I shrugged. "I don't have anything to hide."

He shook his head and held his phone out for me to see.

Spazz: Whose grave was she visiting?

"Oh," I said, understanding why he didn't want to ask. "I don't mind answering that, or any other questions about him. We were visiting Brinkley's father and my late husband, Russell Moore."

He typed a message and placed his phone on the counter, giving me his full attention. "How long's it been?"

"A little over four years."

"May I ask what happened?" he asked cautiously.

I nodded and cleared my throat. I didn't mind talking about Russell, but I hadn't shared that particular story in a long time. "One night after dinner, he said he didn't feel good and went to bed early. He got worse as the night went on, and we eventually went to the hospital. They said he needed to have his appendix removed and started getting him ready for surgery. When they took him back, they sent me to the waiting room. I'd only been in there for maybe fifteen minutes when they came out to get me. He had a reaction to the anesthesia and died before the surgery was even started."

Bear reached across the counter and placed his

hand on top of mine, squeezing gently and giving me the strength to go on.

"It completely blindsided me. The possibility of becoming a widow at the age of twenty-three never crossed my mind. I don't think I would've gotten through it if it weren't for Brinkley."

"How old was she when you lost him?"

"I found out I was pregnant with her two weeks after Russell died." I looked down and shook my head. "I wanted to start having kids right after we got married, but Russell thought we should wait a few years. So we'd just started trying for a baby the month before."

"Damn," he said softly.

"Would you like another cup?" I asked and reached for his empty mug before he had a chance to answer.

I needed a moment to get the emotions I'd inadvertently stirred up under control. But his next words had me turning back to face him.

"I was released from prison nine months ago, after serving sixteen years for killing the man who murdered my wife."

"Why would you go to prison? Weren't you defending her?"

Without an ounce of shame or hesitation, he kept his eyes on mine and said, "No, I was avenging her. I knew who did it when I found her. I hunted him down and tortured him for three days. Then, I killed him."

I'm not sure what kind of reaction he was

expecting from me, but it clearly wasn't the one he got.

"You should've killed him as soon as you found him and then tortured him. If the wounds were postmortem, you would've been charged with body desecration instead of torture and still would have had the same level of satisfaction. Then, you likely could've used temporary insanity as a defense for the murder charge."

He tilted his head to the side and stared at me for several seconds before finally saying, "Since you're obviously not bothered by my past, I'll ask my other question. Why do you know that?"

I pointed to his leather vest. "You're a Blackwing. You wouldn't be one if you weren't a good man. As for the other, I listen to podcasts about court cases when I have trouble sleeping."

"How often is that?"

"Not as often as it used to be but still more than I'd like."

"My daughter-in-law makes this stuff called angel milk when she can't sleep. It's nothing special; just warm milk, sugar, and a splash of vanilla extract."

"Thank you," I smiled. "I'll have to try that sometime."

"You got nothing to lose, because even if it doesn't work, it still tastes really good."

"I'm sure Brinkley would love it. That kid has one hell of a sweet tooth. Maybe we'll have it as a special treat before bed on Christmas Eve."

The pizza arrived a few minutes later. Since I

didn't allow Brinkley to take food out of the kitchen, she practically inhaled her dinner so she could get back to the movie.

"Does she know how to pause it?" Bear asked.

"It's not the same," Brinkley answered from the living room, causing him to laugh.

"Noted."

"Is it time to make the goodies yet?" she asked.

"Not yet," I reassured her and started putting the leftover pizza away.

"Can I help with anything?" he offered.

"Actually, yes, there is something you can do," I said as a brilliant idea occurred to me. "One second." I gathered the ingredients I needed and poured the first two into a large bowl. "Can you mix these two? Then, once they're blended, slowly add this?"

He gave me a curious look, but nodded with a slight grin on his face. "Yeah, I should be able to manage that," he said and proceeded to make my heart happy when he went to the sink to wash his hands first.

Several minutes passed before Bear turned off the mixer and cleared his throat to get my attention. "Do you have something else I can stir this with? If I keep using the mixer, I'm going to burn up the motor. I can already smell it getting hot."

I retrieved a wooden spoon, a spatula, and a large plastic spoon and placed them on the counter. "Take your pick."

He picked up the spatula and went to work on the

mixture. "Did you say all of this?" he asked and pointed to the remaining powdered sugar.

"Yep," I said and quickly turned around to hide the smile on my face. I'd been making the same recipe for years. I was well versed in how difficult it was to mix in the last cup of sugar, which was why I used to pawn the task off on Russell.

"What's next?" Bear asked when he finished with the mixture.

I took it and placed it in the freezer. "This needs to chill for at least thirty minutes before we can do anything with it. But," I said as I reached into the refrigerator, "the dough I made last night is ready to bake."

"What kind of dough?"

"Gingerbread."

"I love gingerbread cookies."

"So do I, but you're not supposed to eat this kind."

"Why not?"

"The recipe's meant for building gingerbread houses. Technically, there's no reason you couldn't eat it, but it's hard as a rock. You could seriously break a tooth."

He laughed and ran his tongue over his teeth. "Thanks for the warning."

We continued talking and making Christmas treats. Brinkley darted back and forth between decorating cookies and watching her favorite Christmas movies.

After she'd been unusually quiet for a while, I

peeked around the corner to find her asleep in the middle of the living room floor.

"She lasted longer than I thought she would," I observed.

"Do you want me to carry her to her bed?" Bear offered.

I shook my head. "She's a sound sleeper. Noises and lights don't bother her. But, if she's moved, she's awake and not going back to sleep for at least an hour. So, I'll get her up a little while before I'm ready to go to bed."

"I should probably get going. I didn't realize it'd gotten so late."

I glanced at the clock on the stove, surprised by the time. It was later than I thought, but I wasn't ready for him to leave. "You have to at least wait until the dirty snowballs are finished so you can take some home. Those cannot and will not stay in my house for any length of time."

He laughed. "Why not?"

"Because I'll eat them. And so will Brinkley. All of them. One time, we finished an entire batch in less than two days. That can never happen again."

"If you don't want to eat them, why do you keep making them?"

I shrugged. "Because I want to."

He grinned. "Good answer."

"Did you hear anything else about the car?" I asked.

"Nothing yet. Spazz is pretty good at what he

does. So, if he hasn't found anything by now, there's probably nothing to find."

"I hope you're right," I said and failed to hide the worry in my voice.

He didn't miss it either. "Let me see if he can give us an update."

I assumed he'd send a text message since that's how he'd been previously communicating with him. However, Bear called him and placed his phone on speaker.

"Hey, Spazz. I'm here with Mackenzie, and you're on speaker. Just checking to see if you found anything before it gets too late."

"Not yet, but I've got a list going of things I still need to look into," he said distractedly.

"Such as?" Bear asked.

"Um, where did I put it? Oh, here it is. Let me see…" he trailed off. "Oh, Mackenzie, do you know if your brothers are still in jail?"

"I only have one brother. My half brother, Tristan. And yes, as far as I know, he's still incarcerated."

"What about Oliver?"

I scrunched my nose in disgust. "Oliver has no blood relation to me. He was my stepbrother for an unfortunate period of time," I clarified. "I haven't checked in a while, but I would assume he's still in prison. The last time I looked, he had several years left on his sentence."

"Thanks, I'll cross their names off my list. What about your other family members?"

"I don't have any."

"None?" Spazz and Bear asked at the same time.

"Other than my daughter, no. If they're not in jail, they're dead or gone."

"Okay, that significantly shortened my list. But so far, I'm not finding anything to suggest a connection between you and Carter Perry. The address on his driver's license is about five miles from your house. Also, his father is buried in the same cemetery as Russell and Nicole."

"So, it makes sense for him to be in the area," I said, but the plausible explanation didn't provide the relief I'd hoped for.

"Looks that way, but I want to look into a few more things before I give you my final report."

"Appreciate it," Bear said. "I'll check in with you tomorrow."

"Thank you," I called out, hoping he heard me before the call was ended.

"Well," Bear said and made his way over to the sink I'd steadily been filling with dirty dishes. "I'm going to help you with these while we're waiting on the dirty snowballs."

I'd been doing the post-holiday baking clean-up all by myself for over four years. So having another adult pitch in was a treat for me, and I couldn't hide my excitement.

"That's the nicest Christmas present anyone's gotten me in a long time," I teased, and ignored the pang of sadness I felt at the truth to my words.

"Not a fan of doing the dishes?" he asked.

"It's one of my least favorite things to do," I confessed. "It's up there with dirty laundry."

He laughed. "I don't mind washing dishes, but I'm with you on the laundry."

"We seem to have a lot in common."

"Yeah, I noticed that too," he agreed, and I could hear the smile in his voice.

With both of us tackling the kitchen, we were finished in no time, and so were the dirty snowballs. And even though I'd gotten him to stay for another hour, I still wasn't ready for him to go.

"I'll never be able to thank you for everything you did today, but I'd like to start with these," I said and handed him a bag with two containers filled with cookies and treats.

He smiled, though I could see the sadness in his eyes. "I should be the one thanking you. This is the most fun I've had in a while."

"Same here. We should do it again sometime," I said before my brain could stop me. "I mean, unless there's a completely obvious reason we shouldn't that I've somehow missed." Like a girlfriend or a wife. I'd assumed he was visiting Batta's mother's grave, but it hadn't occurred to me until that very moment that he could have a significant other. And likely would, considering the time frame.

He covered his mouth in a weak attempt to hide his amusement. "Like what?"

"A woman," I said flatly.

The humor vanished from his face, replaced with understanding. "Ah. There's nothing for you to worry about there," he said and fixed his eyes on me. Somehow, without him uttering a single word, I knew he was waiting for me to verify the same about myself.

"Hey! There's another thing we have in common. I don't have a wife or girlfriend either."

"Think we can go two for two?" he asked without missing a beat. "No boyfriend, no husband. You?"

"No boyfriend, no husband," I laughed.

When Bear opened the front door and came to a sudden stop, the warm and light-hearted atmosphere surrounding us vanished into the cold night air.

I stepped closer and pressed my forehead against his back. "What's wrong?" I whispered, even though I was terrified to hear his response.

"Sorry," he said quietly and placed his hand on my thigh. "Nothing to worry about. Just a little snow."

"Snow?" I blurted and peeked around his side to see my front yard covered in a blanket of white. "When did that happen? Was it supposed to snow tonight?"

"I don't think so," Bear said and continued outside, seemingly unconcerned by the unexpected weather.

"Wait!" I said louder than I intended to, causing my voice to echo through the quiet night. "The roads are probably bad. Why don't you stay here tonight and drive home tomorrow?"

"Brrr!" I shivered and rubbed my arms in a weak attempt to get warm. "Come on, Bear. Even without the snow, it's way too cold to ride."

"Hold that thought," he said and ushered me

back inside the house. "No sense in standing out in the cold when we can discuss the weather and road conditions inside where it's nice and warm."

"There's no sense in you driving home in the freezing cold on treacherous roads when I have an extra bed that's nice and warm."

"Are you sure it's no trouble?"

"It'd be more trouble if you didn't stay. Because then I'd have to stay awake until you got home. And then it'd be another hour or two before I'd be calmed down enough to even think about falling asleep. So really, you're doing me a favor by staying."

"I don't know what kind of mind sorcery you just pulled on me, but I'll let it slide if you promise me right here and now that you will never, ever teach my daughter-in-law any of your tricks."

"I make no promises," I laughed before I yawned and covered my mouth. I was exhausted, but I still needed to move Brinkley to her room. I was standing there weighing the options of risking her being awake for the next hour or two versus leaving her where she was and crashing on the sofa. Either way, my quality of sleep would suffer.

"Have you tried moving her with a blanket?" he asked.

"I'm not sure what you mean."

"Slide a blanket or sheet underneath her. You can use it as a sling to carry her or slide her down the hall to her room."

"Nope, but there's no time like the present to give

it a shot," I said and picked up a throw blanket from the edge of the sofa.

"I can't believe that worked," I said quietly after we successfully moved Brinkley to her room.

"I'm glad it did," he smiled. "My wife was a petite woman, and you've met my son; he was never small."

"I'll definitely be using that trick again," I said, suddenly aware of how close together we were standing in the hallway.

"Well," I said and pointed to the door across the hall. "Here's the guest room. There are some extra pillows and blankets in the closet. And you know where the bathroom is. Let me know if you need anything else."

"Thanks, Mackenzie. I'll be fine."

"Goodnight, Bear," I said and reluctantly closed the door. Even though I was exhausted, I didn't want the evening to end.

4

BEAR

I woke up well before the sun rose and quietly made my way to the kitchen. After watching Mackenzie make coffee the night before, I knew where everything I needed was and helped myself to a cup.

"Good morning, Mr. Bear," Brinkley said several minutes later, effectively scaring the shit out of me.

I jolted in surprise and almost choked on my coffee. "Uh, good morning," I coughed. "You kind of scared me."

"How? I didn't say boo."

"You're right," I laughed. "You didn't."

She climbed into the chair beside me at the kitchen table. "Can you make breakfast?"

I wasn't sure how to answer her. Yes, I was fully capable of making breakfast. For myself. But I didn't know what she could have or if she had any allergies. "Maybe we should wait for your mommy," I suggested.

"Okay," Brinkley happily agreed, much easier than any other hungry child I'd encountered.

I figured out why moments later when she carefully slipped out of her chair and ran down the hall to Mackenzie's room. "Mommy! It's time for breakfast! We're waiting for you!"

Mackenzie materialized several minutes later with Brinkley in tow. "Morning. I hope she didn't wake you."

"She didn't. I've always been an early riser."

"I wasn't, but she is, so I begrudgingly became one."

"Mommy, can we have your crunchy toast for breakfast?" Brinkley asked.

"French toast," Mackenzie corrected. "And yes, you can have it for breakfast." She turned to me. "Do you want French toast, or would you like something else for breakfast?"

"I'm not picky. I'll eat whatever you're making." After the questionable things I'd eaten over the years, I considered anything that wasn't prison food a treat.

While Mackenzie got started on breakfast, I made a cup of coffee and placed it on the counter beside the stove where she was cooking. "Want some coffee?"

She glanced at the mug and back to me before repeating my words from the night before. "I'll never say no to coffee."

"Good answer," I winked and returned to my seat at the kitchen table.

"How's it look outside?"

"About the same as it did when we went to bed. Maybe a little more on the ground."

"I hope it doesn't last long. If I have to drive anywhere today, I'd at least like to do it with a full set of tires."

"I think this will be gone by early afternoon, but I can have a prospect bring over a loaner car from the club until you get your tire fixed."

"Oh, that's not necessary. I don't have anything that has to be done today. I meant if there was an emergency or something."

"We're supposed to go get our Christmas tree today," Brinkley whined.

"I know, sweetie. But we can put up the other decorations today and do the tree tomorrow."

"But Candy won't come until we finish the tree," she cried.

"I'll see what I can do, but I'm not making any promises," Mackenzie said and placed a plate of French toast in front of her daughter.

Brinkley shoved a syrup-covered bite of toast into her mouth as huge crocodile tears ran down her face.

And it damn near broke my heart.

Under the guise of making another cup of coffee, I made my way over to Mackenzie and asked, "Who's Candy?"

"Her Christmas elf," Mackenzie whispered.

"Ah," I said as recognition dawned. After I heard Savior's kids talking about an elf, I asked him about it, and he filled me in on the Christmas tradition. "And the tree has to be decorated in order for Candy to come?"

Mackenzie scrunched her nose. "I think that might be specific to our elf."

I nodded as though I understood, even though I didn't. "I see. Well, the offer still stands. If you'd like to use one of the club's loaners, you're more than welcome to."

She was quiet for a few moments as she considered my offer.

"They sit there and rarely get used, so you'd be doing us a favor," I added. "Plus, it'd be safer for her."

She snapped her fingers and pointed at me. "Well played."

I laughed and dropped a kiss on top of her head like it was the most natural thing in the world. And it was. Until I realized what I'd done. Which happened to be when I looked up and saw Brinkley staring at us before she erupted into a fit of giggles, providing a welcomed distraction.

Drew arrived with the loaner SUV shortly after we finished breakfast. Mackenzie picked up her keys and put on her jacket. "Brinkley, stay in your play area while I move your car seat to the new car."

"I can move it for you," I offered.

"Thanks, but I need to grab a few other things as well," she said. "I'll be right back."

"Stay alert," I mouthed to Drew and nodded toward Mackenzie.

He nodded once and straightened his shoulders

before he turned to scan the area while Mackenzie got her things from her car.

She returned a few minutes later and jingled her keys. "Who wants these?"

"I'll take them," I said and extended my hand.

She dropped them into my open palm as she passed by me on the porch, inadvertently backing into me when she stepped back to open the screen door.

"Sorry," she squeaked and quickly shimmied through the small space, wiggling her firm ass against me as she squeezed by.

I exhaled slowly and tried to focus my thoughts on Drew and Mackenzie's car instead of Mackenzie's ass and my cock.

Fuck it. I tossed the keys to Drew and waited for him to turn toward her car before I readjusted my hard dick. Then, I walked out to her car and gestured for Drew to roll down the window.

With my hands braced on the roof of the car, I leaned down and lowered my voice even though Mackenzie and Brinkley were inside. "Call me if you notice a four-door white sedan tailing you or lurking around at any point while this car is in your possession."

His eyes widened for a moment before he nodded once. "Will do."

"Thanks, man." I tapped the top of the car twice and stepped back to watch him leave before I went back inside.

"Mommy, can Mr. Bear help us get a Christmas tree?" Brinkley asked, tugging on Mackenzie's hand.

"I don't know. He might have a busy day," Mackenzie said.

Since I wasn't sure if she was offering me a way out or if she didn't want me to join them, I put the ball back in her court, so to speak. "Do you need help with the tree?"

"Need it? No. Would I greatly appreciate it? Yes."

"Say no more," I smiled.

When we arrived at the lot, Mackenzie and Brinkley walked around and carefully inspected every single tree, which was quite entertaining to watch.

"Okay, we've got it narrowed down to two trees, but we can't decide. Which one would you pick?" Mackenzie asked and pointed to the two they'd selected.

I blinked once and turned to Mackenzie for clarification. "You're trying to decide between those two?" One was an average Christmas tree, between six and seven feet tall. The other, however, was damn near twice as big.

"Yes," Mackenzie nodded seriously.

I leaned close to her ear and lowered my voice. "The big one. Always pick the big one."

Her beautiful green eyes flicked up to mine as a sly smile appeared on her face. "I want the big one," she said, never taking her eyes off of mine.

Fucking hell. It almost seemed like she was implying something completely different. But I knew better. She was a young, beautiful woman. Of course I found her attractive. I'm sure a lot of people did. But I was much older than her. My son was older than her. So the likelihood of her meaning anything other than the tree was slim to none.

But then again, I loved beating the odds, and I didn't have anything to lose.

"It's right in front of you, beautiful. Go get it."

Her eyes flicked to my mouth while she ran the tip of her tongue over her bottom lip. Then, she looked up at me and held my gaze.

Fuck it.

I'd never been unsure of myself.

And it was too late to start after all the shit I'd lived through.

Wrapping my hand around the back of her neck, I pulled her to me and leaned down to close the distance between us.

"Ma'am, would you like us to net and load your tree?"

Mackenzie flinched and jumped back like a teenager who'd been caught making out. She placed a hand over her chest and turned to the man with an incredulous look on her face. "Am I supposed to know what that means?"

"Sorry," he chuckled. "Would you like us to put a net over the tree and load it into or onto your vehicle? The net helps protect the branches during transport and makes it easier to move inside."

"Uh, yes to both?" Mackenzie asked with her eyes fixed on me.

"Yes to both," I confirmed.

While Mackenzie and Brinkley went to pay for the

tree, I showed him where we were parked and helped him secure it to the roof.

"Wow," Mackenzie gasped and stared at the tree.

"If you think it's too big, we can exchange it for a smaller one."

"No, I want the big one."

* * *

It'd been a long time since I'd had a Christmas tree. And I'd never had one as big as Mackenzie's. As I soon found out, neither had she.

After getting the monstrosity back to her house, we ended up going back to the store to get a different stand for the tree because the one she had was too small.

I didn't realize how long it took us to get the tree moved inside and positioned where she wanted it until I heard a car pulling into the driveway.

"Look, Mommy," Brinkley shouted. "Your car came back."

"That must be Drew," I said and went outside to meet him.

"What was wrong with it?" I asked without preamble.

He shrugged. "They couldn't find anything wrong with the tire. However, she was missing the cap for her valve stem, so they replaced that free of charge."

"Huh," I said and rubbed the back of my neck. Of course, it could've been a coincidence, or someone could've intentionally removed the cover to let the air out of her tire manually. Like someone in a white sedan who parked near her vehicle while she was in the grocery store.

"Anything with the white sedan?" I asked, even though I knew the answer because he hadn't called.

"No," he said disappointedly.

I chuckled. "Hoping for some action?"

He shrugged. "Maybe a little."

"Trust me. It'll happen sooner or later. It always does." I clapped him on the shoulder and pulled him in for a side hug, intending to thank him and send him on his way, when an idea hit me.

"I can't promise any excitement, but I might ask Copper to put a security detail on Mackenzie while I'm looking into something for her. Do you want the first watch?"

"Yes," he answered eagerly, and proudly. "Yes, I do."

"I hope you've got the balls to fill that sack you're swinging."

"Even if I don't, I'm gonna fake it like a boss," he laughed. "When do I start?"

"Not sure. Maybe later tonight or sometime tomorrow. I need to touch base with Spazz and okay it with Copper first."

"Let me know. I'll be around."

"Appreciate it."

Before I went back inside, I called to check in with Spazz.

"Hey, man. You got anything for me?"

He exhaled heavily. "No, and I've pretty much exhausted all avenues."

"Okay, well, that's good news. I'll let Mackenzie know it was probably just a coincidence. Thanks."

"Anytime, Bear."

After we ended the call, I stood outside a little longer. I didn't have any reason to doubt Spazz, but something wasn't sitting right with me. Even though he didn't say as much, I got the impression he felt the same.

When I went back inside, Mackenzie and Brinkley were sitting in the living room floor, trying to untangle a giant ball of Christmas lights.

I held up her car keys. "Good news. There was nothing wrong with your tire."

"Really? Then why was it flat?"

"Not sure. They did say you were missing the valve stem cover, but that really shouldn't have had anything to do with it. Sometimes it just happens."

"Thank you," she said and walked over to her purse. "How much do I owe you?"

"Nothing."

"Bear," she started to protest, but I held up my hand to stop her.

"There was no charge because there was nothing to fix," I explained. She didn't need to know I'd planned on taking care of it for her if there was.

"Also, I talked to Spazz a few minutes ago. He hasn't been able to find anything to suggest Carter Perry might be following you."

"Then, it was probably nothing," she said and

waved her hand dismissively before she quickly looked away. "But I appreciate you both taking the time to look into it."

"Mommy," Brinkley called from the living room, where she was staring up at the tree. "How are we gonna reach the top?"

"Well, Brink, that's a good question."

"Mr. Bear, can you reach the top?"

"Maybe with a ladder," I joked.

"Mommy, do we have a ladder? Mr. Bear needs one to reach the top of the tree," she squealed with excitement. "He can put the star on, and then Candy can come for Christmas!"

Mackenzie sighed. "Is it too late to exchange it for a smaller tree?"

"I was more up close and personal with that tree than I've been with any human in a long time. For that reason alone, yes, it's too late to return it."

"Okay then. Let me go fetch the ladder."

"Is it the one hanging in the garage?" I asked.

"It is."

"I'll get it," I said and brought it to the living room to set up in front of the tree.

"Hold on," Mackenzie said. "I'm going to need food before tackling a project of this size."

"I could eat."

"Can we have McDonald's?" Brinkley asked.

"I don't know about that, but I'll make sure to order something you like."

"Thank you, Mommy. I love you," she smiled and returned to her toys.

Mackenzie laughed. "She must be trying to finagle her way into getting a milkshake too."

I shrugged. "Fast food is fine with me, if that's okay with you."

"It is today. I didn't realize how hungry I was until we started talking about food."

When I offered to pick up the food, Mackenzie grinned and suggested we all go in her car.

Curious as to what was in store, I readily agreed.

When we pulled up to the window to pay for our order, the woman turned to repeat the total and jumped back with a short scream.

"Boo!" Brinkley shouted from the back seat before she erupted in a fit of giggles.

I looked back to see her waving to the cashier, and wearing a hockey mask.

"She's been doing that for about six months now," Mackenzie laughed. "And I have no idea why."

After we had devoured our food, we started decorating the tree. Or we tried to. But the thing was massive. And Mackenzie didn't have near enough lights or ornaments to cover it.

"What am I going to do?" Mackenzie asked quietly after Brinkley had fallen asleep.

"Put the tree topper on and tell her you're finished. Because, technically, you are until you buy more decorations."

"That'll have to work," Mackenzie yawned and sat down on the sofa. "Because I'm too tired to come up with anything else."

5

BEAR

After I left Mackenzie's, I went home and spent the entire night replaying my favorite moments from the weekend over and over in my mind. And even though I couldn't stop thinking about her, I was still completely denying the possibility that I could have developed feelings for her in such a short time. It couldn't be anything more than infatuation. It'd been a long time since a beautiful woman had paid me any attention, and my old ass was likely mistaking her kindness for flirtation.

Even still, I saw no harm in stopping by Mackenzie's the following day to check on her and Brinkley.

I forced myself to wait until after lunch before I rode over to her house.

And I was far more disappointed than I should have been when Mackenzie didn't answer the door. Though, it didn't seem like they were home.

Deciding I would stop back by a little later, I

went to the mall to kill some time and get a jump start on my Christmas shopping. Although I had to admit, I was a little excited about being able to choose the presents myself. Leigh had helped me with that task while I was in prison. But this was going to be my first Christmas as a free man. And after spending two Christmas-filled days with Mackenzie and Brinkley, I had every intention of celebrating it to the fullest.

However, three hours later, the general public had damn near killed any holiday spirit I'd found. The customers were rude, and some of the seasonal workers weren't much better. On top of all that, there was a nationwide shortage of a growing list of items, making a variety of gifts difficult to find.

"Fuck this shit," I muttered to myself and headed for my bike.

"No!" The sound of her shrill scream grabbed my attention as my stomach filled with dread. I knew that voice. "Stop him! He's got my daughter!"

I turned to see Mackenzie chasing after a man running across the parking lot with Brinkley in his arms. She was kicking and screaming as she fought with everything she had trying to get away from him.

Without conscious thought, I jolted into action and ran after them, speeding past Mackenzie in a matter of seconds.

"Let her go, motherfucker!" I yelled.

He didn't. Instead, he picked up his pace.

And so did I. Easily. Because for many years, the only thing I enjoyed and could freely do while I was in prison was work out. And that's why I was able to catch up to them.

When I was within arm's reach, I yelled, "Watch out!" He reacted as I'd hoped and turned to look for the non-existent danger, causing him to slow enough for me to close the remaining distance between us.

I reached out and grabbed the back of his shirt, yanking hard. When he lost his footing, I held on tightly and braced for impact as best as I could.

We hit the ground with a thud, but the unexpected, piercing scream from Brinkley had me freezing on the spot. It was the scream every parent dreaded to hear. The one that meant your child was hurt. Severely.

I pushed myself off to the side as fast as I could to get my weight off of her, only letting go of the asshole who tried to take her for a split second. But it was all the time he needed. Before I could grab him again, he got to his feet and kicked the ever-loving shit out of me before he took off running.

Groaning, I cradled my side and rolled away on instinct, eliciting another shrill scream from Brinkley as she moved with me. Because once I'd gotten a hand on her, I never let go.

"Brinkley! Oh, baby! It's okay! I got you."

"Bear!" Drew yelled, running toward us from across the parking lot.

A sharp pain shot through my torso when I pushed to my feet. "Call the club and stay with them!" I shouted, already chasing after the agile motherfucker.

He rounded the corner of the building and dove into the passenger's side of that fucking white sedan, which was conveniently running and waiting for him.

The moment he was inside, the driver hit the gas and took off, headed straight for me.

"All right, fuckface. Let's do this," I said and widened my stance. I'd never lost a game of chicken, and I'd be damned if I'd start with this asshole.

6

BEAR

"The fuck, Dad?" my son yelled in surprise when I kicked open the front door to the clubhouse several hours later.

"Sorry, my hands are full," I said and tossed my prize onto the floor. "Take that down to the basement for me, would you? I need to check on my girls."

After several seconds of Trey staring at me with the same look of fear he had on his face when I returned after avenging his mother's death, I firmly cupped his cheek with the palm of my hand. "Nothing to worry about, boy. I didn't kill him this time. Now, get moving. And where are the girls?"

"They're in the room beside yours," Copper answered. He came to a stop beside Trey and looked down at the pathetic man on the floor. "Looks like Santa brought us a present early. Who wants to play with it first?"

"Make sure there's some left for me," I called over my shoulder, already on my way to Mackenzie's room.

As I was coming down the hall, Drew knocked on the door, whispered something I couldn't hear, and then turned the knob to push it open. "She's been waiting for you," he said quietly. "And Brinkley's asleep."

"Thanks," I said and squeezed his shoulder before I stepped into the room, closing the door behind me.

I heard her coming and turned around just in time to catch her as she launched herself into my arms. I dropped my hand to her ass and lifted. She wrapped her legs around my waist and buried her face in my neck. "Bear," she gasped against my skin. Then, I felt her entire body shudder as she started to cry. "Thank you," she whispered, digging her nails into my shoulders. "Thank you, thank you, thank you."

Carrying her into the bathroom, I sat her on the counter and kept my arms wrapped tightly around her. "How's Brinkley? Is she okay?"

"Yes," she nodded and sniffled against my chest. "She's got a few bumps and bruises, but nothing major. The doctor said she'd be okay, but," she paused when her voice hitched. "I don't know how much she understands or will remember about what happened today."

"Somebody tried to take my baby," she cried. "She's all I have. They can't have her!"

She had me; she just didn't know it yet. But, she would. Soon.

I didn't try to soothe her with placating words.

Instead, I held her against me and let her share her pain with me.

After several minutes, when her tears had subsided, she pushed back suddenly and pinned me with an angry glare. "And where in the hell have you been?"

With my arms still tightened around her, I leaned forward to drop a kiss on top of her head before I told her the truth. "I was out catching the son-of-a-bitch."

Her head shot up while her mouth gaped open. "You caught him?" she whispered.

"Fuck yes, I did."

"What did you do with him?" she asked worriedly.

"Brought him back here for the boys to lock up in the basement," I explained and stepped back to turn on the water. "I wanted to check on you two and get a shower first before we decide what to do with him."

While the water was heating up, I hung my cut on the door and pulled my shirt off over my head.

"Bear," Mackenzie gasped seconds before her cold fingers touched my side.

"Holy shit, woman. Why are your damn hands so cold?" I joked, trying to cover the way I flinched at her touch.

I hadn't looked at it myself, but I knew there had to be a nasty bruise from where I'd hit the ground earlier.

"You need to have this looked at."

I twisted my torso and glanced at my side in the mirror. "Well, shit," I grumbled. Not only was a massive bruise already visible, but I had a nice chunk of road rash too. "Yeah, it might not hurt to have Splint take a look at it."

She placed her hand on my arm. "Bear?"

"Yeah?"

"Are you gonna kill him?" she whispered.

"Do you want me to?" I asked. He tried to take her child. He did take her. So what if he was stopped before he made it out of the parking lot? I still had no problem getting rid of him.

She bit her bottom lip while she considered her answer. "I don't want you to get in trouble."

Ah. Like the last time. "Listen, when I killed the man who murdered my wife, I was well aware of what I was doing. I knew I would end up serving time when all was said and done. I didn't regret it then, and I don't regret it now. But," I said and held up one finger when she opened her mouth to speak. "This is different."

"How so?"

"I knew you'd be waiting for me to come back," I confessed before I covered her mouth with mine.

She pressed her body against mine and threaded her fingers through my hair, fisting it tightly. Lifting her by her ass, I hoisted her onto the countertop. As I continued to devour her mouth, I gripped the hem of her shirt and slid it up her torso, breaking the kiss long enough to pull it over her head and toss it to the floor. Or that's what I intended to do until my eyes landed on her beautiful bare tits.

"Fucking gorgeous," I said and lowered my head

to suck her nipple into my mouth while I used my fingers to tease the other one.

When I stepped back, she propped herself up with her arms and watched me curiously, her breasts rising and falling with each breath she took.

I undid my belt and let my jeans drop to the floor, never breaking eye contact while I kicked them to the side.

Palming my hard dick, I stepped forward and reached for the waistband of her jeans. When she lifted her hips, I wasted no time in yanking her pants down her legs, along with the panties she was wearing.

I'd inadvertently pulled her close to the edge of the counter. When she moved her feet to push herself back, her legs widened, giving me the perfect view of her bare, smooth skin. Without warning, I dropped to my knees and buried my face in her pussy.

"Bear!" she gasped loudly and slapped her hand over her mouth, trying to stifle her moans while I ate her pussy like a bear searching for honey.

I wasn't anywhere near finished when she started begging me to stop and fuck her instead.

"Please, Bear," she groaned. "I need your dick."

Needed it.

And I needed her to have it.

With one last hard suck on her clit, I moved up her body and slid my arms around her, pulling her against me so I could carry her to the shower.

When our bodies came together, my lips met hers, and my cock notched right at her entrance.

Mackenzie canted her hips forward while she pressed against my ass with her heels, pushing my dick to the hilt inside of her. And then she lightly tugged on my bottom lip with her teeth.

"Fuck me, Bear," she whispered.

And that was it.

I tightened my arms around her and abruptly stood, holding her against me while I walked to the shower. Stepping inside, I pressed her back against the wall and slid my arms under her thighs. With her legs draped over my elbows, I stepped back to bring her ass off the wall.

And then I moved. I didn't wait—for her, for me, for any fucking thing. I held her hips in place, pulled back, and thrust forward, fucking her at a hard, steady pace.

She came within a minute or two, begging me to fuck her harder while she did.

And I happily obliged.

But as the walls of her tight pussy rippled around me, I hit the point of no return. I bit down on her shoulder to stifle my groan as I came from something other than my hand for the first time since before I went to prison.

I stepped closer and pressed her against the wall, kissing her while keeping my cock buried deep inside of her.

She shifted her hips, inadvertently squeezing my dick when she did. Or so I thought. But after she did it a few more times, I broke the kiss and moved my mouth to the shell of her ear. "You want me to fuck you again, baby?"

She nodded against me and wiggled her hips.

"Say it."

"I want you to fuck me, Bear," she said with zero hesitation. Then, she brought her hands up to cup her breasts while she teased her nipples. "Now, please," she sassed.

I pulled out of her and placed her on her feet, making sure she was steady before I turned her around. Cupping her tits from behind, I lightly pinched her nipples. "I really want to spank your ass for that."

I grinned when she crossed her legs and pressed back against me as she squirmed.

"You want that, don't you, baby?" I asked, running one hand over her ass cheek and squeezing.

"Yes, please," she breathed.

"Put your hands on the wall and stick that ass out."

She did as I said and glanced back at me over her shoulder, nodding once as if to say she was ready.

I smoothed my palm over the curve of each cheek before I reached up and covered her mouth with my hand, seconds before I landed a hard slap to her wet ass cheek. Even stifled by my hand, her yelp was loud enough for someone to possibly hear.

"Shhh," I reminded her. "I don't give the first fuck who knows what we're doing in here. But if you do, I suggest you keep it down."

I didn't give her any warning before I slapped my

palm onto the opposite cheek. Mackenzie jolted forward but managed to contain any audible reaction.

"Unless you like being watched," I mused as my hand drifted between her legs. Running my fingers through her slit, I knew I'd find her soaking wet from our previous activities, regardless of how she felt about being watched. But I enjoyed teasing her.

She made a noise of frustration when my fingers skipped over her clit, giving me an idea. "Spread your legs wider for me."

I wanted to laugh when her legs popped open immediately, thinking I was ready to fuck her again. And I would be. Later.

"Nice," I praised and smoothed my hand over her cheeks once more. "Since you've been a good girl so far, I'll let you choose—six slaps to your pussy, and we're finished. Or I spank your ass while you play with yourself until you come."

"Oh, shit," she panted and moved one hand to her hip. "The last one."

"Say it."

She heaved in another breath and pushed her ass out even more. Then, she looked over her shoulder and winked. "I want you to spank me until I make myself come."

I watched in awe as her fingers appeared between her legs and slipped inside her core. She moved them in and out a few times before she started circling her clit with her wet fingers.

I only thought I was hard before. My dick swelled until it was damn near painful as I watched

Mackenzie play with herself, my red handprints prominently displayed on her pale, white ass.

"Fucking hell, woman," I groaned and pressed my throbbing erection against her hip in a futile attempt to get some relief. All the while, I added more of my handprints to her pert little ass at a steady rhythm. The same rhythm I was going to use to fuck her the moment she came.

It was less than a dozen slaps later when she gasped and arched her back. I gripped her hips and lined myself up with her entrance, pushing inside when she started to orgasm. She bit down on her fist and shoved her ass back, meeting me thrust for thrust while she rode out the waves of her pleasure.

Fucking hell. It wasn't long after her orgasm subsided when I felt the familiar tingle in my balls, much to my disbelief. There was no way I was going to come again so fast. There hadn't been enough time.

"Bear," she gasped. "Please don't," she started and slammed her mouth shut while she closed her eyes and tilted her head toward the ceiling. "Oh, fuck. Please, don't stop."

It was then I noticed she still had her hand between her legs, furiously circling her clit. When she started to come, it felt like the walls of her pussy were massaging my dick with each pass. I continued pounding into her. She froze, and her entire body briefly tensed as tremors ran down her arms and legs while her release washed over her. And I followed right behind her.

We hadn't even had time to separate when I heard someone tapping on the other side of the shower wall. "Yoo-hoo," Tatum sang. "The guys are in the hall arguing over who has to be the one to interrupt y'all's love fest to tell you there's news you need to hear. You're welcome."

Then, a few seconds later, she tapped the wall again. "We will never speak of this. That is all."

"Fuck," I groaned and stepped back so I could turn Mackenzie around and lift her into my arms. Dropping my forehead against hers, I gently kissed her lips. "I'm not anywhere near finished with you."

"Promise?" she teased and moved her body against mine.

"Fuck yes," I said and squeezed her ass for good measure before I placed her on her feet.

"Let me go see what this is about," I told her while I dried off and got dressed. Then, I handed her my phone. "Keep this."

"Why?"

"So if this is gonna take a while, I'll have to come back and find my phone." I wrapped my hand around her neck and brought her to me. "And then I'll fuck you while we're 'looking for it.' Because I'm not waiting more than a few hours to be back inside of you."

"Holy shit, Bear," she breathed.

"Yeah, I know," I said and kissed her once more before I opened the door and stepped into the empty hallway. "Be ready for me when I get back."

I made a mental note to thank Tatum for clearing

everyone out. Like I'd told Mackenzie, I didn't give the first fuck what the brothers heard or saw as far as I was concerned. But I didn't expect her to automatically have the same comfort level I did. Plus, I'd been in prison. I could shit in front of a stranger and smile the whole time.

"In here," Copper called out as I passed by Church on my way to the common room.

"Whatcha got, Prez?" I asked and dropped into a chair. The adrenaline rush I'd had was long gone, and I could feel the soreness creeping in.

"Little fucker started singing before we even touched him," Copper shared without a drop of humor.

"Why does it sound like that's not great news?" I asked cautiously.

He sighed and rubbed his chin with his thumb and forefinger the same way his father and grandfather used to do. "Because it isn't. The man we have downstairs is Sean, Carter Perry's son."

"Yeah," I nodded as he shared information I already knew and gestured for him to continue.

"Carter was arrested a few months ago and is currently behind bars awaiting trial."

"Okay," I said slowly, failing to see how any of that was bad news.

"Daddy Perry's girlfriend is Mitzie Mayfield, Mackenzie's mother," Bronze blurted.

I pushed back from the table and got to my feet. "The fuck did you just say?"

"According to Sean, they started dating about a

year ago, and she moved in with Carter a couple of months later. When Carter was indicted on federal charges a few months ago, most of his assets were frozen, leaving Mitzie and Sean on a tight budget. So when Mitzie randomly spotted Mackenzie and Brinkley out shopping, she got the bright idea to kidnap Brinkley and hold her for a hefty ransom."

"What? Where did she think Mackenzie would get that kind of money?"

"I'm assuming from us."

"Why would she think that?" I asked, feeling like I was missing something.

"We've dealt with Mitzie before."

"When the fuck did that happen?"

"About a year before you were released," Trey clarified.

I inhaled deeply and blew it out slowly as another thought occurred to me. One I didn't want to acknowledge but couldn't ignore either. "When I asked Mackenzie about her family, she said they were all dead or in jail," I explained and waited for one of them to answer my unasked question.

Did she lie to me?

Coal straightened in his seat and leaned forward on his elbows. "You sure that's what she said?"

"Those weren't her exact words, but it was something like that. Why?"

"Because we told her if anyone ever asked about her family, she should specifically say, 'If they're not in jail, they're dead *or* gone,' and change the subject."

"Why would she say that to me? I'm a Blackwing."

"She probably thought you knew. Or maybe she thought you were testing her. Besides, we didn't tell her how we handled things with her mother," Copper added.

"Well, tell me."

"Basically, after all was said and done, we told Mitzie if she disappeared, her problems with us would too," Copper said.

"And if she reappeared?"

"So would we."

"Well, hocus pocus, motherfuckers. Let's make this cunt's problems reappear," I said and headed for the door.

"Wait," Copper called out, stopping me in my tracks. "You stay here and let us go get her."

"You can't be serious?" I asked incredulously. Someone fucked with my woman; therefore, I had to handle it personally. It was expected. He fucking knew that.

"Okay," Copper nodded. "Who do you want to be the one to hold Mackenzie while she cries after they tell her her own mother is the one who arranged to have her daughter kidnapped?"

"Point made," I acknowledged. "I'll be in my room. Let me know when you get back." The sooner I was gone, the sooner they could leave.

"No need," Tatum announced as she walked into Church like she had every right to be there. Then, she tossed a bound and gagged Mitzie onto the floor. "But

I agree with him." She nodded to Copper. "You need to be the one to tell Mackenzie. Take your time. I'll stay with Mitzie until you get back."

"How did you?" I asked, letting my words fade while I gestured to the woman on the floor.

"I'll explain later," Tatum started.

"Give me the short version now," I insisted.

"I was there. At the mall. I saw everything happen. Since the scene was secure, I followed you."

"Why?" I asked, even though I was pretty sure I already knew what her answer would be.

"In case you needed help. I'm not about to let you go back to prison after we just got you out. Not if I can help it," she said quietly.

I stared at her in disbelief.

"When you went after the guy, I went after the woman. I would have been here sooner, but I could hear her rolling around in the trunk, and well, I was having a little too much fun with that."

I turned to my son and waited for him to at least pretend to try to do something about his woman.

He laughed and held his palms up. "I ain't saying shit. She saved me from having to go track down that bitch."

"Consider it an early Christmas present," Tatum said with exaggerated sweetness and puckered her lips for a kiss. "I love you, baby."

"I love you too, my badass pain in the ass."

"Do you think you two lovebirds can preen over your prey in the basement? The rest of us have shit to do."

"Go ahead, Papa Bear. We got this," Tatum said.

I whirled around and tapped the tip of her nose once with my finger. "No," I said sharply and walked out of the room, knowing she couldn't follow me without breaking her promise to stay with Mitzie.

"He just," Tatum huffed, and I swear I heard her stomp her foot. "He booped my nose."

"Will it make you feel better to boop someone's nose?" Trey asked.

"Don't you fucking—" Copper stopped abruptly.

"It did!" Tatum squealed. "One more time! Boop!"

Holy shit. My son had his hands full with her.

I lightly knocked once on the door before I turned the knob and let myself in. Mackenzie was obviously pacing the length of the room and stopped mid-step when she saw me. "How is she?" I whispered and pointed to Brinkley.

"She seems okay. She hasn't woken up, and she doesn't seem to be uncomfortable. What was the news?" she asked without preamble.

I took her hand and led her through the bathroom and into my room on the other side. "Drew's still stationed outside the door. He'll hear her if she wakes up."

"Just tell me," she said softly but firmly.

I sighed and pinched the bridge of my nose. "Carter Perry's son is the man who tried to kidnap Brinkley. And he was working with your mother."

"What?" she gasped before rage replaced her momentary surprise. "Where is she?" she growled and started to pace the room again. "We have to find her. Because I'm going to kill her."

I placed my hand on her shoulder. "Your mother's here."

"You got her?"

"I got him. Someone else got her."

"Thank them for me." She inhaled deeply and met my eyes. "I want to see her."

"Why?" I countered. "What are you gonna do?"

She blinked up at me. "I don't know. I'll figure it out when I get there."

"Hang on, baby. Take a minute and think about what you're saying. What you're doing. You've got time. She's not going anywhere. That, I can assure you."

Mackenzie came to a stop and took a seat on the edge of the bed, dropping her face into her hands. "My mother has never been any kind of mother to me, but I," she paused and shook her head. "Why would she do something like this? To her daughter? To her granddaughter?"

"Money," I said simply.

She snorted derisively. "Well, that's not surprising. She's always strived to live off of other people's money. How much was my daughter worth?" Before I could answer, she held up her hand to stop me. "No. Don't tell me."

She remained quiet for a few minutes longer before she came to a decision. And once she did, she nodded resolutely and rose to her feet. "I want to talk to her."

"You sure?"

She smiled, but it wasn't friendly. "Yes, there's something I want to say to her."

I extended my hand for hers, ready to stand by her side while she faced the woman who should have been focused on making her dreams come true, not creating her nightmares.

The moment we headed for the door, the determination in her eyes vanished. "Wait. Where are we going? I don't want to be far from Brinkley."

I didn't either, but if Mackenzie wanted to see her mother, I was going to be with her. And we damn sure weren't taking Brinkley with us. "Coal," I blurted. "He's here. He can stay with Brinkley while we go downstairs. You okay with that?"

"He'll come and get me if she wakes up?"

"No, he'll stay with her and send Drew."

"Even better." She inhaled deeply and squared her shoulders. "Okay, let's do this."

Coal arrived moments later to stay in the adjoining room with Brinkley. "We won't be gone long," she told him and looked to me for confirmation.

"Take your time. I won't go anywhere until one of you comes back," he promised. "If she so much as stirs, I'll send someone to get you."

"Thank you, Coal," Mackenzie said sincerely.

"Any time. That's my little buddy in there," he said and placed his hand on Mackenzie's shoulder. "And you're my friend."

"She's one of us," I added and led Mackenzie

away before either of them could comment on the declaration that slipped from my mouth.

We stopped in front of the door to the basement. Before I entered the code to unlock it, I turned to Mackenzie and asked one last time, "You sure?"

"Oh, yeah," she said, her fierce determination burning bright once again.

After we descended the stairs, I pointed to the door to the room where Mitzie was being held. "She's in there whenever you're ready."

Mackenzie turned the knob and entered the room without a moment's hesitation. She crossed her arms over her chest and glared at her mother.

"How much were you hoping to get for my daughter?" she demanded.

"I should've known you'd be here," Mitzie sneered.

"How much?"

"I didn't want to be greedy, so I was only gonna ask for twenty-five thousand," Mitzie said with exaggerated exacerbation.

I don't know what I expected to happen next, but it wasn't Mackenzie leaning forward and laughing so hard she had to brace herself. "Oh," she exhaled and wiped the tears from underneath her eyes as she tried to regain some composure. "This is like a fucked up version of that Christmas story with the gifts. But instead of selling something of yours to get something for me, you stole my daughter to get something for yourself!"

"I did not steal your daughter," Mitzie snapped.

Mackenzie narrowed her eyes and slowly nodded her head. "You're right," she acknowledged. "You tried."

"What do you want from me?"

"There was a time when I did want something from you. But that time has long since passed. If you'd tried to be any kind of a mother to me, instead of trying to fuck your way through life, you'd have everything you always wanted. Instead, you're locked up in a basement waiting on a motorcycle club to decide your fate."

Mitzie rolled her eyes and held up her bound wrists to talk with her hand. "Blah, blah, bullshit."

"All I wanted was a mother. I really needed a mother when I lost my husband. And again when I delivered his daughter nine months later. But all you ever wanted was money." Mackenzie's smirk turned into a deviously proud smile. "Here's where you fucked up. When I received the payout from Russell's life insurance, I invested it wisely. Now, I have what you've always wanted, and you've got," she paused and used her thumb to point to the brothers lining the wall behind her, "problems."

Mitzie's mouth started to drop open before she quickly slammed it shut.

"Hundreds of thousands, 'Mom'. It didn't even occur to you, did it?"

"Mackenzie, hun, let's talk about this," she started. Then, her eyes widened, and she pointed her finger toward several of the brothers. "Blame them!

It's their fault I wasn't there for you. They told me I had to stay away."

"Nice try," Mackenzie said. "But that happened well after Brinkley was born."

"I'm sorry, hun. Momma's always loved you. I just don't always show it so good. Please, baby, give me another chance. I'll get it right this time," Mitzie begged.

"Shut her up," I ordered and pointed to my son.

Trey stepped forward and raised his bat in the air. When he started to swing, I moved my eyes to Mackenzie's face and waited for the sound of impact, but it never came. And neither did the recoil I expected from Mackenzie.

I turned to see Mitzie's head slumped to the side as my son smoothed a piece of duct tape over her mouth.

"I wasn't going to actually hit her," Trey said disappointedly. "I was just gonna scare her a little before I covered her mouth, but she fucking passed out and stole all my fun."

"It's okay. I've heard similar bullshit from her over the years," Mackenzie said, directing her attention to me. "It doesn't matter what she says; I won't fall for it."

"If there's anything else you want to say to her, we can wake her up," Trey offered and produced a vial of smelling salts from his pocket.

Mackenzie smiled appreciatively. "Thank you, but I said all I needed to say."

I put my arm around her shoulders and leaned

down to whisper in her ear. "Do you care at all what happens to her?"

"Would it make me a bad person if I said no?" she asked with genuine concern in her voice.

"Not by the standards of anyone in this room," I told her honestly.

"As long as I don't have to worry about her being a problem for us ever again, I don't care how that happens."

"I'll take care of it," I told her and walked her back to Brinkley.

"She hasn't made a sound the whole time," Coal whispered when we entered the room.

I turned to Mackenzie. "I'm not sure how long I'll be, but if you need anything, let Drew know. He'll be outside the room until I get back."

Mackenzie circled her arms around my waist. "Be careful."

"Nothing for you to worry about, baby," I assured her and placed a kiss on the top of her head.

When I returned to the basement, I was damn near giddy with excitement. I'd forgotten how much fun I used to have in my prime days as the Enforcer for the Blackwings. And I was suddenly eager to make up for lost time.

I clapped my hands once and rubbed my palms together as if I was trying to warm them. Then, I looked back and forth between Mitzie and Sean. "'Tis the season to die, bitches. Who wants to go first?"

The sound of someone knocking on the door at

the top of the stairs had me pausing. And then rolling my eyes when they continued incessantly knocking.

"Who the fuck is that?" Copper muttered.

"I think we know who it is. The better question is, what the fuck does she want?"

I knew as well as they did Tatum wouldn't interrupt unless it was urgent. Quite frankly, I was shocked she was even still in the building. She didn't know exactly what we were doing, but she knew enough to know it wasn't something she should be around for.

Trey quickly ascended the stairs and opened the door. I listened intently but couldn't hear anything they were saying. A few moments later, Trey jogged down the stairs with an unreadable look on his face. He went straight to Copper and whispered something close to his ear. Copper's eyes widened briefly before he inhaled deeply. "Church!"

Once we were upstairs behind closed doors, Copper slid a cell phone that'd seen better days across the table to Spazz but addressed the room. "That's Mitzie's cell phone. The last few messages she received were from an unknown number. They start out asking for an update on the package and become more aggressive, demanding to know where she is and when she'll arrive."

Spazz already had the phone in his hand while his fingers tapped away at the screen.

"Sorry, she's going to be late. She's a little tied up at the moment," Trey laughed, as did the rest of the guys.

"Shit, that one never gets old," Judge chuckled.

"Hold on. What package?" I asked and glanced between Copper and Spazz. "What fucking package?" I demanded and stood from my seat.

"I'm guessing Brinkley," Spazz announced with his eyes still glued to the phone. "I don't know the who, what, or why yet, but she was definitely supposed to take an important package to another person."

"Do you have any idea who this person is?"

"No, not a clue," Spazz said distractedly. "But I'm working on it."

Copper nodded and focused on me. "You and Batta go downstairs and see if you can get anything out of Sean or Mitzie while Spazz is doing his thing. Whoever she was supposed to meet will likely be looking for her or their package. We need to know what kind of loose end we might be dealing with."

Fuck! The possibilities were endless. And I couldn't let myself go down that sick and twisted rabbit hole. Not until I was given the okay to spill blood. Then, I'd do my worst.

I inhaled deeply and squared my shoulders. "Come on, boy. Let's do this."

I entered Sean's cell without preamble and grabbed him by his throat, continuing forward until the back of the chair he was tied to hit the concrete wall, as did his head.

"Please don't kill me. Please don't kill me," he begged.

"I ain't promising shit," I spat and tightened my grip around his neck.

"I'll do whatever you want. Just please don't kill me," he cried.

An image of Brinkley's tear-streaked face as she screamed and reached for her mother over Sean's shoulder flashed in my mind, and my vision blurred with rage.

"Bear," my son said from behind me. He'd never called me by my road name before, and it was enough to bring me back to my senses.

I glanced over my shoulder. "Yeah?"

He chuckled and nodded to the floor. "It's easier for him to talk if he's conscious."

I looked down at the pathetic piece of shit on the floor, sniveling through the blood trickling from his nose and mouth.

"Yeah, but this makes me feel better," I grumbled and reluctantly put the chair back on its feet.

"Watch your step."

I looked down and chuckled as I stepped over the puddle of piss.

"One second," Trey said and stepped out of the room. He returned moments later with something in his hand. "Use this. It makes clean up a lot easier."

I took it from him but had no idea what it was. "The fuck is this?"

"Disposable underwear," he said proudly.

I shook my head and tried to hide my smile. "This must've been your idea."

"It was," he said and tossed me a pair of gloves. "But wait until you see what Judge came up with. Help me get his pants down."

"Say what now?"

He laughed. "I know what you're thinking. I was thinking the same thing when Judge first showed it to me. But just wait."

He spent the next few minutes attaching some contraption to the poor fucker's nutsack.

"All right," he said when he was finished and looked to Sean. "We're gonna ask you some questions. If you tell us what we want to know, you'll be just fine. But if we don't like your answer or you refuse to answer, this little baby right here is going to send electric pulses straight to your junk. And the juice goes up each time. Ready?"

"No! Fuck no. I'll tell you whatever you wanna know, man," Sean blurted as he squirmed around in his seat.

"For the sake of your balls, I sure hope so," Trey said and looked to me.

"What were you gonna do with the kid?"

"I already told those other guys," he said.

"Wrong answer," Trey said and pressed the button.

I struggled to contain my amusement when Sean let out a high-pitched yelp of pain.

"I'm sorry! Fuck, man!" Sean blurted. "I was just supposed to grab her and get her to the car."

"And then?"

"I don't know. She said the kid was her granddaughter," he said between breaths. "She said her daughter would be able to get the money as long as the kid wasn't hurt."

I snatched the controller from my son's hand. Then, I pressed the button and sent a jolt of electricity directly to Sean's balls.

"The kid was hurt," I growled.

"She wasn't supposed to be! Mitzie said it was all set up. The mother wasn't supposed to fight me. And then you came out of fucking nowhere."

"What'd you just say?"

Sean's eyes widened comically as he began to panic. "I don't know! Shit, fuck! Please, don't shock my balls again."

"About the mother," I prompted.

"She wasn't supposed to fight me. Mitzie said she'd let me grab the girl and run so she wouldn't get hurt and we wouldn't draw too much attention."

"You're saying Mackenzie knew this was going to happen?"

"That's what Mitzie told me. She said it was fine as long as the girl wasn't hurt."

I knew for a fact that wasn't true. Mackenzie would never have even considered it. What I didn't know was if Sean was lying to us or if Mitzie lied to him.

"What was the rest of the plan? If you had gotten her?"

"I swear I don't know. She told me to grab her and get to the car. That she'd handle the rest of it and get the money."

"Tell me something, Sean. You ever heard of a kidnapping working out like that? The bad guys get away with the money and the child goes home unharmed?"

"No, but this was different. It wasn't a real kidnapping," he insisted.

I crossed my arms and met his eyes. "It was a real kidnapping. The mother knew nothing about it. And the local police are currently trying to find you."

"You're lying."

"Why would I lie to you?"

"To make me look guilty so you can kill me."

I chuckled. "I don't need a reason. If I want your life, I'll take it."

Sean started slowly shaking his head. "You're saying Mitzie lied to me?"

"I'm saying the mother wasn't in on it."

"She lied," he mumbled to himself as he tried to process this new information. "Why would she lie to me?"

"Would you have done it if the mother didn't know?"

"Fuck no," he answered immediately.

"Well, there's your answer."

Sean stared at me blankly for several seconds before he closed his eyes and dropped his head. I'd seen it many times during my incarceration—the moment someone realized they'd been swindled.

"That fucking cunt," he seethed. "She set me up."

I shrugged. "Kinda looks that way."

"I swear I didn't know."

"So you've said." I held up my hand to stop him before he could say it again. "We know Mitzie was planning on taking the kid to someone. Find out who and why, and we'll see what we can do for you."

"You serious?" he asked hopefully.

Trey and I both laughed. "Oh, you ain't getting out of here unscathed by any means, but if you help us out, you're less likely to leave here piece by piece."

"I'll do whatever you want," he vowed, and for some reason, I believed him.

7

BEAR

We moved Sean and Mitzie into the only room in the basement with a camera and headed upstairs to watch the show with the rest of the brothers. The live camera feed was already streaming on the large television mounted on the wall.

"Did we miss anything?" I asked and took my seat at the table.

"Not yet," Bronze answered.

"You fucking lied to me!" Sean yelled. "Your daughter didn't know shit about your plan, and now the bikers think I was actually trying to kidnap your granddaughter."

Mitzie wrinkled her nose in disgust. "You mean my daughter's daughter. Granddaughter makes me sound like a grandma."

"It won't matter what you sound like if you're dead. They're gonna kill us, Mitzie. Kill. Us. Now, tell me what the fuck is really going on."

She rolled her eyes and tilted her head toward the ceiling, exhaling heavily. "They're not gonna kill us."

"Yes they are!" Sean screamed and made all four legs of the chair come off the ground when he tried to stomp his feet. "Do you see the blood on my face? Does it look like they're joking around?"

Mitzie stared at him with an unreadable expression while he took a moment to catch his breath.

"You need to start talking," he seethed.

Mitzie shook her head and made a show of clamping her mouth shut.

"If I'd gotten the kid, we couldn't have gone back to the house, and we couldn't ride around in the car, so where were we going?"

"I got nothing to say."

"Of course you don't," Sean said with disdain. "Let me lay this out for you. The bikers know your daughter wasn't involved, and they know you were meeting someone. They're gonna find out who that was one way or another."

"I don't care what they think they know."

"I want to know! What were you supposed to do with the kid?"

"I don't know. Whatever I was told to once the ransom was paid."

"What about before you got the money? What were you going to do with her until then?"

Mitzie narrowed her eyes. "Why the hell do you care? All you had to do was get her, and you fucked that up!"

"Because I don't want to fucking die! Stop being a cunt for five seconds so we can get out of this mess."

"Whatever."

"If you tell them where you were taking the kid, they said they'd let us go."

Mitzie's eyes widened and she tried to lean forward, giving Sean her full attention. However, the restraints securing her to the chair prevented her from doing so. She looked down at the rope around her waist for several seconds before she cut her eyes back to Sean, seeming to consider her options. "They said that?"

Sean nodded eagerly. "Yes!"

She laughed. "You're dumber than I thought if you believe them."

"Really? You're not going to at least try to save our asses?"

"No, I'm not. If they were going to kill us, they would've done it by now," Mitzie said confidently. "They're just trying to see what they can get out of us before they hand us over to the cops. They did the same thing with my son and stepson."

"You'd rather go to jail than walk away free?"

Mitzie smirked. "Why would I go to jail? I didn't do anything wrong."

"You were driving the getaway car."

"As I recall, I came to pick you up from the mall and someone was chasing you across the parking lot. You jumped in the car, and I drove away. I didn't know you were running from a botched crime."

"Botched crime?" Sean shouted. "It wasn't

supposed to be a crime. You said your daughter was in on it."

"I don't recall saying anything like that."

"Oh, so this is all just one big coincidence? You really think anyone's going to believe that?"

"I don't know what you're talking about. I thought you were being chased by some crazed holiday shopper. I had no idea what was going on."

"The fuck you didn't. You're the only one who does know what's going on."

"I guess that makes it my word against yours," she said with confidence she shouldn't have.

"So you weren't planning on meeting someone after you got the kid?"

Mitzie whipped her head in Sean's direction with a look of utter shock on her face. She quickly masked it, but not before everyone watching saw it, including Sean. "No," she huffed. "Why would you even think that?"

"Because it's fucking true," Sean said flatly.

"It is not."

"I'm just saying, if you were planning something with someone, now'd be the time to place all the blame on them. You seem to be pretty good at that."

"I ain't blamed anyone for anything."

"You're blaming me right fucking now! Like you're completely innocent in all of this."

"I am completely innocent."

"Bet my dad would disagree."

Mitzie narrowed her eyes and studied Sean. "What's that supposed to mean?"

"It means exactly what you think it means."

"You don't know anything," Mitzie said weakly.

"That little shit was holding out on us," Trey whispered.

"I don't know. I think he's bluffing." And I did. By the way Sean was blubbering and sharing everything he had to share to save his ass the moment he could made me think he'd told us all he knew.

"I know enough to save my ass and leave yours in its place. And yes, Mitzie, they are going to kill you. Why wouldn't they? No one's looking for you, and no one's going to miss you."

"Your dad will."

"My dad hates you."

Mitzie's eyes widened in shock. "What?" she asked in disbelief.

"You heard me. He hates you. Which means there's a reason he's keeping you around."

"You know why he keeps me around."

"It's not for your dried-up old cunt," Sean laughed. "It was to keep tabs on you because he knew what you were up to."

Mitzie tried to shift in her seat and glanced around the room nervously.

Sean leaned as close as he could to Mitzie and lowered his voice. "Even you're not stupid enough to try kidnapping a kid with no guaranteed ransom."

"Those bikers would've paid the ransom," she insisted, but Sean ignored her words and continued on.

"Where were you taking the kid?"

Once again, Mitzie pressed her lips together and shook her head. I might have laughed at her display if they weren't talking about the precious little girl who'd stolen a piece of my heart in the short time I'd known her.

"Come on, Mitzie. Think about it. If I can figure it out, it won't be long before they do. And then you've got nothing to bargain with."

When Mitzie remained silent for several minutes, Sean continued. "You're the only one who can get us out of here and clear my dad's name. Then, he'll owe you."

"So what? He doesn't have shit. That's how we got into this mess to start with."

"Yeah, but when the charges are dropped, he'll get everything back." Sean paused and lowered his voice. "And if he can prove my grandfather was murdered by his wife, he'll have even more."

"Fucking Pamela," Mitzie blurted.

"What was that?" Sean asked.

"Pamela. All of this is her fucking fault. If she would've just given me the money I asked for, we wouldn't be sitting here."

"She flipped quick! Did y'all see that?" Bronze laughed.

"What money?"

Mitzie rolled her eyes. "I asked her for the money to pay our rent. She went on and on about how she'd already paid me, and how I wasn't gonna get any more money out of her. I was like, 'After everything I've done for you, you won't help me out?' That's when she told me about the other job."

"The other job?"

"She wanted me to bring her a kid."

Sean made a sound of disgust and turned his head away from Mitzie.

"Right? I was like, 'No fucking way. That's disgusting, and I don't want nothing to do with it.' But then she said it was just for pictures. Of the kid. By themselves. So, I thought, okay, that's not so bad."

"Not so bad? You're fucking sick!"

"I didn't do anything wrong. I was just the middleman."

"Holy shit! Have you done this before?"

"What? No! Of course not. But desperate times call for desperate measures."

"Yeah, like staging a fake kidnapping to get some money from the local vigilante bikers. You said nothing about kiddie porn!" Sean heaved in a breath and looked directly at the camera mounted in the corner of the room. "I swear to fuck I didn't know."

Mitzie followed Sean's eyes and gasped when she noticed the camera. "You stupid son of a bitch!!" she screamed and began to thrash against her restraints.

Sean, however, slumped back in his chair with a look of utter defeat on his face. I almost felt sorry for him. Almost.

Before I had a chance to give it any more consideration, Copper's phone rang, drawing all eyes in the room to him. He glanced at the screen and exhaled heavily. "Somebody other than Batta and

Bear go separate those two fuckwads. I have to take this." With that, he stepped away from the table and raised his phone to his ear.

I remained seated and shamelessly tried to overhear what was being said to him. Unfortunately, I couldn't make out any words, but I recognized the voice almost immediately.

Tatum.

And she was in business mode. Which couldn't be good, considering she was well aware of what was going on at the clubhouse.

Copper ended the call quickly and whispered something to Spazz as he returned to the head of the table.

His eyes landed on Trey first, and stayed there. "That was your wife with some developing news."

Spazz turned his laptop toward Copper. "This is live," he said quietly.

Copper's eyes widened as he studied the screen. "Can you put that up there for everyone to see?"

"Yeah, but it'll replace the camera feed."

"The footage is still being recorded, right?"

"Yes, and saved in two locations."

"Go ahead."

Moments later, the screen filled with live coverage of breaking news.

"If you're just now joining us, we are at the home of Pamela Perry. Several months ago, the body of her husband, Carter Perry, was found floating in a body of water on the property. The death was ruled an accidental drowning. Tonight, another body has been found floating in the same pond. We're told this is being classified as a homicide investigation."

"Tatum doesn't know who the victim is, but she did say it's not Pamela Perry. She's trying to find out more on her end without raising too many flags. But, she's made a connection between here and there. And it won't be long before others do too."

"What connection?" my son asked.

"Mitzie," Copper answered immediately and cleared his throat. "Tatum suggested we tend to our guests sooner rather than later."

Copper turned his attention to Spazz. "You got anything yet?"

"Oh yeah," Spazz said proudly. "Pamela Perry, née White, married Carter Perry, Sr. two years ago. According to the reports, Mr. Perry drowned while he was out fishing in a pond on his property. Toxicology results found alcohol, sleeping pills, and anti-anxiety medications in his system. His death was ruled accidental. But here's the thing, his son is adamant that's not what happened."

"People get drunk and drown all the time," Copper pointed out.

"Not people who don't drink," Spazz said flatly. "Or fish."

Copper gestured with his hand for Spazz to continue.

"There's a good bit to sift through, but his son has been relentlessly trying to prove Pamela was involved in his father's death from the get-go. In Carter's statement to the police, he tells them his father abhorred alcohol to the point he wouldn't even allow it in his home. His statement also claims his father didn't care for any kind of fishing."

"What was Carter Perry, Sr.'s net worth at the time of his death?"

"A little over four million, including properties and other assets."

"Pamela was the sole beneficiary?"

"Yep. No prenup, and he updated his will after they were married. Everything went to her."

"Well, there's motive right there, but Pamela's responsibility for her husband's death doesn't have anything to do with us. I need to know if there's anything besides Mitzie and Sean that does."

"Got it, Prez," Spazz replied while his fingers continued to move over his keyboard.

"Time isn't on our side this time, brothers," Copper said. "We've got to get this shit wrapped up quickly and efficiently. Suggestions?"

Judge leaned forward on his elbows. "You said 'one of the ponds.' How many are there?"

"Four."

"Do we know which one has the body in it?" Judge asked.

A map of the property appeared on the screen, and Spazz used his cursor to point to the pond in question.

"What are you thinking?" Copper asked.

"Maybe the son is on to something. And even if he isn't, I don't see why we can't make his theory work for us. We give Mitzie a special cocktail and leave her floating face down in the pond. Regardless of her involvement, Pamela will have plenty of questions to answer after another body appears in one of her ponds with the exact same cause of death. And it'll keep anybody from putting us under a microscope for a while."

"Won't the property be crawling with law enforcement? How are we going to nonchalantly drop a body in a pond without being seen?" Savior asked.

Copper gestured to the map still on the television screen. "We're going for this one right here. It's the farthest from the house, and we can access it from the highway. The time it takes us to change the flat tire we're about to have will be more than enough to slip her into the pond. Spazz, can you pinpoint an area that isn't covered by any traffic cameras?"

"Already have," he replied and zoomed out on the map on the screen. "You're clear from here to here."

Copper nodded. "That'll work."

"What about Sean?" I asked. I didn't want to admit it to my brothers, but I wasn't so keen on spilling his blood after interrogating him, especially after watching his interactions with Mitzie. In short, I believed his story. And as much as I wanted to kill anyone who hurt Brinkley or Mackenzie, I wasn't sure enough of his guilt to assuage mine.

Copper leaned back and rubbed his chin in the way all the men in his family did when they were pretending to think. "Well, I'm not sure about him, and we don't have the time to be sure right now. But I know someone who can keep an eye on him and keep him out of our hair while this dust settles."

"Boar?" I asked with a smile on my face.

"Boar," Copper confirmed.

"I'll make the call. Batta, Bear, Splint, and Coal will stay here with Mackenzie and Brinkley. Tiny, Grant, and Drew will take Sean to Boar's club. And the rest of us will get rid of this bitch once and for all. If shit goes tits up, call Tina, and then call Uncle Tommy. No one says a word without one of our lawyers present."

"I understand why I'm staying here, and I'm not arguing with your decision, Prez. But, since I can't kill her, can I at least be the one to drug her?" I asked.

Copper cracked a smile and shook his head, but a laugh still escaped him. "Yeah, man, go right ahead."

"Appreciate it," I said and rose to my feet. "Come on, boy, let's go see what this old hag wants for her last drink."

* * *

SURPRISINGLY, MITZIE DIDN'T EVEN HESITATE WHEN I placed a glass of whiskey in front of her. She downed the contents the moment I freed her hand. She placed the empty glass on the table and asked, "Can I have another?"

That's when I noticed her hand trembling. "You an alcoholic?"

"Yes, she is," Sean said as he passed by the door with Grant and Drew.

"When was your last drink?" I asked her.

"Right before that bitch jumped me and brought me here."

"That bitch is my daughter-in-law," I said.

"My apologies," she said, not bothering to hide her sarcasm.

I shook my head to myself and sighed. If Mitzie was already showing signs of withdrawal in the few short hours she'd been at the clubhouse, it was going to take more than one glass of whiskey with a few crushed pills in it to knock her out.

It took five, though the last two were whiskey only. I didn't want her to die before she was supposed to. She was already catching a break by getting to go out in a drunken stupor. But she didn't deserve to die without suffering a little. I also didn't want her to puke and fuck up all of our plans.

Somewhere between the third and fourth glass, she started to talk.

"I know you put something in my drink. I can feel it."

I smirked. "That's okay. The important thing was that you didn't taste it."

"Why?"

"You know the answer to that."

"So it's like that?"

"I'm not sure why you thought it wouldn't be."

She sighed. "Well, if I'm going out, I'm taking Pamela with me."

"How are you planning on doing that?"

"By telling you all of her dirty little secrets."

I laughed. "This ought to be good. Let's hear it."

"Pamela Perry paid me to date her stepson and plant evidence in his house to make it look like he was the one involved in producing and selling child pornography."

"You're saying he wasn't?" I asked, unsure if I should believe anything that came out of her mouth.

She nodded and took another sip of her drink. "Yep, that's right. Everything Carter told the police is true. Pamela married his dad for his money and his land. She killed him when he found out about her side hustle. And then she framed Carter to make sure she got everything."

"What about Sean? He's not a threat to the inheritance?"

Mitzie snorted. "I don't know how all that shit works, but I'm guessing he is because he's up next on her list." She leaned forward and lowered her voice, "So if you kill him, you'll be doing her a favor."

"You got any proof what you're saying is true?"

"Talk to Carter. He'll tell you his dad called him the day he died and asked him to meet him the next day for lunch. Said he needed to talk to him about something in person." She placed her empty glass on the table. "You get more when I get more."

I filled her glass and gestured for her to continue.

"His dad thought Pamela was having an affair and hired a PI to investigate. He must've been pretty good, because he found out about Pamela's studio hidden on the property. And that's what Carter's dad wanted to talk to him about."

"And how do you know any of that?"

"Because I was in the car with Carter when the PI called after his dad died. I heard every word he said."

"If the PI found the studio, then how did Carter end up in jail instead of Pamela?"

"Because she killed his dad and paid off the PI."

"Do you have any proof?"

She snorted a laugh. "Do you think I would be sitting here if I had proof of all the shit she's done?" She finished the remainder of her drink and gave me an expectant look.

"What's the PI's name?" I asked while I refilled her glass.

"Brian Sullivan or something like that. I know his last name started with an s because Pamela thought it was hilarious that his initials were B.S."

I nodded and waited for her to continue. But she didn't. Her eyes were starting to droop, and it was clear she wasn't going to be coherent much longer. So, I took the opportunity to ask a question I hoped she would answer honestly, though I was taking anything that came out of her mouth with a grain of salt. "What about Sean?"

"What about him?"

"How involved in all of this is he?"

She exhaled heavily and seemingly tried to focus. "He didn't know anything about it until today."

"What about the kidnapping? Did you tell him it was staged?"

"Does it matter?" she slurred.

I shrugged. "Not to me. But I'm sure it does to him. And maybe his father."

She nodded. "Yeah, you're right about that. Carter only cares about two things: his son and his money."

"Sounds like he cared about his dad."

"He did, but his dad's dead."

"About that. How do you know Pamela was behind his death?"

"Because she made me help her do it."

"Made you?"

"Made me. Paid me. Whatever."

"And Sean?" I prompted.

"Sean's an idiot," she said as her head lolled to the side. "And he fucks like he sparkles." She raised her head, looked me directly in the eyes, and opened her mouth as if she was going to say more, but fell forward face first onto the table before she could.

Once I was sure she was out cold, I helped the boys load her into the back of Copper's truck. Bronze climbed into the passenger seat while Judge and Savior got into the back on either side of Mitzie.

"If we're not back in an hour, start making phone calls," Copper said and clapped me on the shoulder.

"Hold on a sec, Prez. I don't know why I didn't think of it before, but what do you think about having Sean put Mitzie in the pond? If he gets caught, it wouldn't be too far-fetched for the two of them to be on the property. Especially with this in his pocket." I handed him a bottle of whiskey that was half empty and had a few crushed pills in it, the same ones I'd given to Mitzie. "And if he gets away with it, we'll have some leverage to use while we figure out what to do with him."

"I like it. I'll explain it to the boys on the way," he said and walked around to the driver's side of his truck. "Tiny!" he called out. "Change of plans. Y'all follow me. I'll call you with the details in a few minutes."

Copper returned his attention to me. "Better give us an hour and a half to get back. He won't be near as fast as us."

"Got it, Prez," I said and stepped back to watch as they drove away with a trailer full of motorcycles, two criminals, and one blown tire, hoping like hell they could pull it off.

I knew I was too keyed up to wait for their return with Mackenzie. Not without disturbing Brinkley. I don't care what Mackenzie said, there was only so much noise a child could sleep through, and there was no way we wouldn't wake her with the way I was feeling.

So, I went down to the basement and made sure there was absolutely no trace of Sean or Mitzie in the clubhouse. Then, I went through the rest of the clubhouse. By the time they got back, the entire place was damn near spotless.

"You weren't worried, were you?" Copper asked with a hint of a smile.

"Nope, not at all," I lied and crossed my arms over my chest while I waited for one of them to fill me in.

"Everything went according to plan," Copper said, finally putting me out of my misery. "I assume Mackenzie will be contacted by the police as next of kin once the body is discovered."

"Do you think it would be better if she wasn't here when that happens?"

"If she's yours," he said and gave me a knowing look, "it'd be suspicious if she was anywhere other than here after what happened earlier today."

"Then here is where she'll be."

EPILOGUE

BEAR

Christmas Eve

After Brinkley's attempted kidnapping, Mackenzie and I hadn't spent a single day, or night, apart.

Thankfully, Brinkley seemed fine. She talked about her "boo-boos" while they were healing, but she hadn't said a word about what caused her injuries.

"Can we open presents now?" Brinkley asked excitedly.

"We can open presents as soon as everyone gets here," Mackenzie said. "Correction. We can open presents a few minutes after everyone gets here."

"Okay," Brinkley sighed and plopped down on the floor in her poofy Christmas dress. But the disappointment she projected seemed excessive, even for the promise of toys.

"What's wrong, doodlebean?"

Before she could answer, the doorbell rang.

"They're here!" she jumped up and ran to the door.

"Freeze!" Mackenzie called out.

Brinkley raised her hands in the air. "I wasn't gonna open it."

"I got it," I said and opened the door for Trey and Tatum.

"Merry Christmas!" Brinkley cheered and waved excitedly.

"Where should we put these?" Trey asked.

"The tree's right through there."

"Holy mother—"

"Little ears!" I blurted to interrupt my foul-mouthed daughter-in-law.

She narrowed her eyes and continued, "—of all trees."

Mackenzie laughed. "You should've seen Bear's face when I said that's the one I wanted."

"I'm glad they didn't see yours when you got the big one you wanted," I rumbled close to her ear.

She turned toward me to hide her face and playfully slapped my chest. "Not in front of the kids."

"You realize my son is older than you, right?"

I jumped back when I felt something pinch the skin on my lower back. "Ow!"

Mackenzie held up her hands in surrender. "What? Wasn't me."

"Is everyone here, Mommy? Can we open presents now?" Brinkley asked again.

"Hang on," I said and squatted down to her level. "I need Trey to help me with your Mommy's present," I whispered.

"Can I help too?"

"Yes, you can show Mommy and Tatum your new Christmas dance while we're getting the present," I suggested.

She nodded with determination and marched into the kitchen. "Want to see my Christmas dance?" she asked and twirled around without waiting for their answer.

I nudged Trey with my elbow and motioned for him to follow me outside.

"More presents?" he asked when I came to a stop beside my truck.

"Sort of," I said and leaned against the door, crossing my arms over my chest.

"I hope you're not about to ask me if it's okay for you to be with Mackenzie," he said vehemently.

"Well, I was," I said slowly, unsure of how to interpret his response.

"Dad," he sighed and took a moment to choose his words carefully. "I know what it's like to lose a parent. So, the only thing I want for the one I've still got is for him to be happy. If that's with her, then let me know when I can welcome her to the family."

I unlocked my truck and reached inside to retrieve the small black box from the center console.

"Well, I suppose you can in about five minutes," I said and held up the box for him to see. "If she says yes."

As we walked back to the house, Trey asked, "Do you want us to clear out for a few minutes?"

"Listen, son. I'm old. I say what I've got to say, and I don't give a shit who's around to hear it."

With that, I walked into the kitchen and wrapped my arm around Mackenzie, pulling her against my side.

"They're back! Time for presents!" Brinkley announced.

I placed the box on the counter and turned to face Mackenzie. "We both know the value of time with our loved ones. I know it's fast, but I don't want to waste any time. You may not be ready for this step yet. And that's okay. But I want to make sure you know what my end game is. I'm in this for the long haul. I love you, and Brinkley. I want to get married and be a family."

She flicked her eyes to the box, then back to me. "What if there's one more?" she whispered.

When my forehead wrinkled in confusion, Mackenzie moved my hand down to her stomach.

"Are you—?" I asked, needing her to say the words I never thought I'd hear directed at me again.

"I'm pregnant," she breathed.

"Put the fucking ring on, woman," I growled.

"Okay," she said and reached for the box while I took her lips in a soft kiss.

"Well, Dad?" Trey asked from the living room with Brinkley in his arms. "Am I getting a little sister for Christmas?"

"Maybe. Or it could be a little brother. It's too early to know," I answered.

"Way to steal our thunder, Grandpapa Bear," Tatum huffed. "Not a word, old man. Pregnancy hormones do some wicked shit," she grumbled and pointed to the unshed tears in her eyes.

"Mommy, what does pregnancy mean?" Brinkley asked.

"Time to open presents!" Mackenzie announced.

Over an hour later, the presents had been opened, and the living room was covered in wrapping paper with Brinkley somewhere in the middle playing with her new toys.

"Brinkley, come say bye to Trey and Tatum before they leave."

"But we're not finished opening presents."

"Yes we are," Mackenzie told her gently.

Brinkley jumped to her feet and darted behind the Christmas tree. A few seconds later, she poked her head around the side. "There's one more! Be right back!"

She rummaged around behind the tree, jostling the ornaments as she did. "Here it is!" she announced and proudly carried a flower to Mackenzie. "It's for you and Bear. Merry Christmas!" she said and smiled so widely it made my face hurt.

"Thank you," Mackenzie said while she bent down to hug her daughter. "That was very sweet of you."

"It's from Daddy and Mystical."

"From who?" Mackenzie asked with a hint of alarm in her tone, which had me instantly on edge.

"From Daddy and Mystical."

"Who's Mystical?" Mackenzie asked slowly.

"The pretty lady with the pretty flowers who lives near Daddy."

"Miss Nicole," I said softly.

ALSO BY TEAGAN BROOKS

Blackwings MC - Croftridge

Dash (Blackwings MC Book 1)

Duke (Blackwings MC Book 2)

Phoenix (Blackwings MC Book 3)

Carbon (Blackwings MC Book 4)

Shaker (Blackwings MC Book 5)

Badger (Blackwings MC Book 6)

Croftridge Box Set

Christmas In Tinsel Town

Blackwings MC – Devil Springs

Copper (Blackwings MC – Devil Springs Book 1)

Judge (Blackwings MC – Devil Springs Book 2)

Savior (Blackwings MC – Devil Springs Book 3)

Batta (Blackwings MC – Devil Springs Book 4)

Bronze (Blackwings MC – Devil Springs Book 5)

King Mountain Shifters

Slade (King Mountain Shifters – Book 1)

Standalone Novella

Beached

ABOUT THE AUTHOR

Website
www.teaganbrooks.com

Facebook Author Page
https://facebook.com/teaganbrooksbooks

Reader Group
https://www.facebook.com/groups/tbbooks

Society6 Store
https://society6.com/teaganbrooks

Printed in Great Britain
by Amazon

57598807R00066